JOHNNY GRUELLE

ORPHANT ANNIE STORY BOOK

MAJOR CONTRIBUTING SUBSCRIBER

LAUGHNER BROTHERS AND FAMILY

Orphant Annie Story Book

Text and Illustrations

by Johnny Gruelle

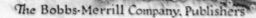

The Bobbs-Merrill Company, Publishers

New edition September, 1989, Indiana Center for the Book, Inc.
an Affliliate of the Library of Congress Center for the Book
This facsimile edition is printed with the permission of Macmillan Inc., 1981.
Distributed by Guild Press of Indiana, 6000 Sunset, Indianapolis, IN 46208

Library of Congress Number: 89-808-52

ISBN   0-9617367-9-8

Original Engraving Done by Stafford Engraving, Indianapolis

Contributing Subscribers For This Edition

Lincoln National Corporation

John and Barbara Wynne   N. K. Hurst and Company

INTRODUCTION

The ORPHANT ANNIE STORY BOOK was written and illustrated by Johnny Gruelle, the creator of Raggedy Ann, as a tribute and memorial to his dear friend and neighbor James Whitcomb Riley and to his own beloved little daughter Marcella, both of whom died in 1916. Marcella's short life had been much gladdened by Riley's fascinating characters and colorful poems.

Richard Gruelle, Johnny's father, achieved lasting fame as a Hoosier artist. At the age of twenty-two, Johnny went to work at *The Indianapolis Star*, as an artist and cartooonist. The Gruelles lived at 506 Lockerbie Street and Riley at 528. Lockerbie Street today is much as Mr. Riley described it, "a dear little street, nestled away from the noise of the city and the heat of the day."

The ORPHANT ANNIE STORY BOOK, first published in Indianapolis in 1921 by the Bobbs-Merrill Company, describes the famous Annie as sturdy and capable at "earning her keep," but with a flair for fantasy that delights those who listen to her tales. At the same time, the stories in the book reveal the simple and basic truths that form her philosophy for a happy life.

Johnny Gruelle died in 1938. Probably neither he nor Mr. Riley realized that the creation of Orphant Annie was not only the creation of a character, but of a concept so appealing to human nature and so basic to human compassion that she continues to beguile each generation in some form or another—as a doll, in a Little Orphan Annie comic strip or even on the stage as the President's adviser.

The Indiana Center for the Book and the many enthusiastic people who have made possible the rebirth of this beautiful book, truly a Hoosier literary classic, wish the reader many happy hours. May you always cherish the memory of "Little Orphant Annie" born in the "rhyme-haunted raptures of Lockerbie Street."

LITTLE ORPHANT ANNIE *

By James Whitcomb Riley

LITTLE Orphant Annie's come to our house to stay,
  An' wash the cups an' saucers up, an' brush the crumbs
    away,
An' shoo the chickens off the porch, an' dust the hearth, an'
    sweep,
An' make the fire, an' bake the bread, an' earn her board-an'
    keep;
An' all us other childern, when the supper-things is done,
We set around the kitchen fire an' has the mostest fun
A-list'nin' to the witch-tales 'at Annie tells about,
An' the Gobble-uns 'at gits you
            Ef you
                Don't
                    Watch
                      Out!

Wunst they wuz a little boy wouldn't say his prayers,—
An' when he went to bed at night, away up-stairs,
His Mammy heerd him holler, an' his Daddy heerd him
    bawl,
An' when they turn't the kivvers down, he wuzn't there at all!
An' they seeked him in the rafter-room, an' cubby-hole, an'
    press,
An' seeked him up the chimbly-flue, an' ever'wheres, I guess;
But all they ever found wuz thist his pants an' roundabout:—
An' the Gobble-uns 'll git you
            Ef you
                Don't
                    Watch
                      Out!

An' one time a little girl 'ud allus laugh an' grin,
An' make fun of ever' one, an' all her blood an' kin;
An' wunst, when they was "company," an' ole folks wuz there,
She mocked 'em an' shocked 'em, an' said she didn't care!
An' thist as she kicked her heels, an' turn't to run an' hide,
They wuz two great big Black Things a-standin' by her side,
An' they snatched her through the ceilin' 'fore she knowed
      what she's about!
An' the Gobble-uns 'll git you
            Ef you
                  Don't
                        Watch
                              Out!

An' little Orphant Annie says when the blaze is blue,
An' the lamp-wick sputters, an' the wind goes *woo-oo!*
An' you hear the crickets quit, an' the moon is gray,
An' the lightnin'-bugs in dew is all squenched away,—
You better mind yer parunts an' yer teachurs fond an' dear,
An' churish them 'at loves you, an' dry the orphant's tear,
An' he'p the pore an' needy ones 'at clusters all about,
Er the Gobble-uns 'll git you
            Ef you
                  Don't
                        Watch
                              Out!

IN MEMORY OF

JAMES WHITCOMB RILEY

who knew the child-mind and delighted in
its every fanciful imagining; who was himself
a child at heart, a player of make-believe, a
dweller in fairyland.

Indebted to the great Hoosier for guidance
and inspiration, another and a lesser Hoosier
has long felt a compelling desire to show
through the making of some such volume
as is here offered in dedication, his deep
appreciation and his abiding affection.

Johnny Gruelle

ORPHANT ANNIE
STORY BOOK

I

WHEN ORPHANT ANNIE CAME TO CARL AND BESSIE'S HOUSE

THE day Orphant Annie came to Carl and Bessie's house, the children were down on the floor in front of the great fireplace looking at picture books.

The morning had started out with a cold drizzling rain, but later had turned colder, so that the drizzle became a filmy curtain of snow. Not enough, however, to make the ground white, except in patches here and there. Toward noon the mud in the roadway began to freeze, and the wind, sweeping across the wide meadows, whistled about the house and made the shutters bang and squeak. As every one knows, who lives in the country, a passing wagon or buggy is an object of curiosity. Those who are in the back of the house rush to the front windows to see who it may be. So when the sound of rickety wheels drew near and a buggy stopped in front, Carl and Bessie jumped up from their cozy place before the fire and ran to the front window, while Mother came from the kitchen to join them. As they gazed they saw Father come around the side yard from the barn, walk slowly out the front gate and up to the buggy.

A tall, round-shouldered man lifted a thin, poorly clad girl over the wheel and put her into Father's outstretched arms, much the same as if he were lifting a shock of corn. Mother drew the children close to her as they all watched with keen interest the scene at the front gate. After a few words to Father, the strange, round-shouldered man pulled his coat collar up close about his bearded face, jerked on the lines a time or two, gave the horse a smack with a 'lath and, without so much as a backward glance, disappeared slowly down the muddy road—he and his horse and his rattly old buggy.

As Mother turned from the window she pressed both children to her and knelt down with her face close to theirs, and when she got up to open the side porch door for Father, Bessie saw that she brushed a tear from her cheek.

Carl and Bessie followed Mother to the door and stood wonderingly aside as Father stomped in with the little girl in his arms.

"Well!" he cried cheerily, "here we are at last! Now we'll soon be warm and cozy! Won't we, Mother?" And with this, Father walked across the room and put Orphant Annie on the sofa.

Then as Father seemed to have done all there was for him
to do, he blew his nose loudly and went out to finish his work
in the barn.

Mother, however, untied the green veil that held Orphant
Annie's hat on her head and unpinned the tattered shawl from
around her shoulders. The children looked at the newcomer
with eager curiosity and they saw that she must be very cold.
Her little hands were covered with mittens, made from old
stockings, that were so short they left the thin wrists showing
bare and blue. Orphant Annie's shoes, as the children after-
ward learned, had belonged to her aunt and were so large
they could easily have held feet twice the size of Orphant
Annie's, while the toes turned up just as do the toes of the shoes
worn by Turkish women.

When Mother went to the kitchen to get something warm
for Orphant Annie to eat, Carl picked up her hat and looked
at it. It was a funny, old summer hat with a bunch of faded
flowers twisted about the crown and held in place with heavy
black linen thread.

During all this time Orphant Annie seemed frightened
and her large eyes moved restlessly from one to the other
of her new-found friends, as much as to say that she was not
accustomed to such kindness. But when Mother came back

3

with large slices of buttered toast and a cup of hot tea, Orphant Annie's eyes never once left the tray until the toast and tea had vanished. Then as Mother sat beside her on the sofa, Orphant Annie told them that the man who had "brung" her was Uncle Tomps. "An' I'm awful glad I'm come!" she said a bit shyly. " 'Cause!" she added when asked for her reason, " 'cause Uncle Tomps and Aunt 'Lisbeth don't live here! But they'll be droppin' in often, ef you don't watch out!"

Uncle Tomps and Aunt 'Lisbeth had "let" Orphant Annie out to work "fer her board and keep," and the little girl, soon on happy terms with the household, thrived on the "board and keep" and proved a willing, cheerful, hearty worker.

But to Carl and Bessie, Orphant Annie seemed to have come direct from the Land of Fairies, and they grew to love her as they would if she had been a Fairy Godmother, such as Cinderella had.

Orphant Annie was a strange, mysterious, fancy-filled little girl, who delighted the children continually with her songs and stories, her games and riddles. While at her work and alone, except for Carl and Bessie, she would often talk to make-believe playmates until the children could almost see the imaginary characters.

At such times, the children were content to watch and listen, for as she spoke to her make-believe friends, Orphant Annie always answered for them in a changed voice to suit the person she pretended she was talking to, and she seemed to forget that the children were in the room.

"Toot! Toot!" Orphant Annie cried as she rattled the dishes. "Here she come! Stand back from the platform there, little boy! Do you want this train to run over you? Chug, chug, chug! Sweeeeeeeeeee!" and Orphant Annie made a noise like an engine when it first starts. "Hello! Here comes the Conductor! Mr. Conductor, is this the train for

Orphant Annie

Greencastle?" Then in a gruff voice: "No, lady, this is the ten forty-five for Indianapolis."

"Oh, dear!" Orphant Annie went on, but now in the thin quavering voice of an old lady, "I wanted to go to Greencastle!" The children could see the old lady with her shawl pinned about her stooped shoulders and a little black bonnet tied on her white head, while there before her stood the big Conductor with all his shiny brass buttons and his blue and gold cap.

"Well, I'll tell you what, Missus, we'll change this train to run to Greencastle instead of Indianapolis! Get aboard there and you'll find a seat right by the third window. That's it! There you are!" Then as the children imagined the conductor helping the little old lady on the train, Orphant Annie turned and cupped her hands as if shouting a long way down the train. "Hey, Bill!" And Bill answered from way off where he sat in the engine cab, "Whatcha want?" "Turn the train 'round, here's a nice ole lady wants to go to Greencastle 'stead of Indianapolis!" the Conductor answered. "Aw right," came back from Bill, sitting up in his cab window way down at the head of the train. Then with a cry from the Conductor of "All aboard!" Orphant Annie picked up an armful of dry dishes and with much chug, chugging and shuffling of feet, turned the train around and sent it to Greencastle while she herself carried the dishes and arranged them in the cupboard.

Many accidents happened on the trip, which lasted until all the dishes were wiped and placed on the shelves.

As the last cup was put away, the train whistled and came to a stop, and the Conductor helped down the old lady, who promised to remember him in her will.

"There!" said Orphant Annie, her eyes dancing. "Le's go in and play the organ and sing songs!" And with their arms about her, the children went skipping from the kitchen.

II

THE GNOME OF THE APPLE TREE

WHILE good food, and plenty of it, filled out Orphant Annie's thin little body and kindly treatment brought a gypsy-like rosiness to her cheeks, she still retained a certain fairy kind of wildness which at times was beyond the understanding of the older people.

To Carl and Bessie, however, she always seemed a creature you would expect to see peeping out from behind deep woodland bushes; one whose place was with Gnomes and Elves as they formed their Fairy Rings and danced in the shimmering moonlight.

If anything, Orphant Annie's large brown eyes grew more luminous and more mysterious as her body grew in health, so that at times the children felt sure that Orphant Annie saw more than they could see.

And, when Orphant Annie found Carl and Bessie keenly delighted with her weird stories of Fairies and Goblins, she was always ready and able to account in a fairy way for whatever happened about the farm.

Carl and Bessie's love for Orphant Annie was mixed with a wonder that was beyond their childish understanding, and the longer she lived with them, the more their wonder grew

7

until they fully expected she might vanish some day before their very eyes.

To the children, Orphant Annie might have passed through a keyhole had she wished, or she might easily have done any of the magical things she told them of in her stories. Not that Orphant Annie said she might do these things, but because the children felt that she really belonged to Fairyland and had the powers that Fairies are supposed to have.

Carl and Bessie came out upon the back porch where Orphant Annie was busy peeling potatoes, and sat down on the long step beside her.

"You should have been out here just a moment ago!" said Orphant Annie. "Then you would have seen him!"

"Who?" the children asked.

"Why, the little Gnome of the apple tree!" Orphant Annie replied, as she turned the potato in her hand and cut a curl of the paring at least three feet long. "Isn't that a daisy!" she laughed, as she bounced the long curl up and down.

At another time perhaps the children would have been interested in the curl of potato-peeling, but now they wished to hear about the Gnome of the apple tree.

"Did you see him?" Bessie asked.

"Oh, you mean the little Gnome! I had forgotten!" laughed Orphant Annie. "It isn't every time that I can peel a whole potato without breaking the curl! It's a sign of good luck when you can do that, or else you will find a hidden treasure, or a pocketbook filled with money that doesn't belong to any one."

At the side of the woodshed there stood an old apple tree, gnarled and twisted in all the agony of apple trees, and at the bottom of the trunk there was a hole large enough for an ordinary sized cat to crawl in and out.

"Did the little Gnome go into the hole in the apple tree?" Carl asked.

"No, he just came out and went across the meadow," Orphant Annie answered. "Oh pshaw! I broke that one!" she added, as another long curl fell in two pieces.

Carl and Bessie walked down to the apple tree and took turns looking up into the hole, but it was so dark inside they could see nothing.

Orphant Annie went on peeling the potatoes and paid not the least heed to the children until they came again and sat on the steps beside her. Then, as if it were quite natural for them to know, she said, "Yes, he's lived there ever since the tree was knee-high to a grasshopper."

"How do you know, Orphant Annie?" Bessie asked.

Orphant Annie looked at her in surprise, but did not tell how she knew.

"When that apple tree was a teeny weeny apple tree," said Orphant Annie, "the little Gnome lived over in a great oak in the woods. He was a very kindly little fellow and whenever any of the other woodland folk were in trouble, he would always help them as much as he could. When Mrs. Bunnikin's rabbit babies ate bitter toadstools, the little Gnome ran over to the Bunnikin home and gave them just the right kind of medicine, so their fat little stomachs would not ache. Indeed

9

he was always doing kindly acts for all who lived in the great woods."

"Just how large is the little Gnome, Orphant Annie?" Carl interrupted.

"He really is very cunning!" Orphant Annie replied, closing her eyes slightly as if the better to recall his image. "He's just about twelve inches high and has a little red beard that reaches nearly to his waist. He wore a green coat when he came out of the apple tree a minute ago, and yellowish brown knee-breeches and white stockings. His hat is shaped like a pine cone and is green too."

"Oh! I'd love to see him!" both the children cried.

"It's really quite hard to see him when he stands perfectly still!" Orphant Annie told them. "The green of his coat and hat is a queer grayish green and sort of blends into the color of the grass or the tree trunks."

"Why did he leave the woods and come to live here on our place?" Carl wished to know.

"I was just coming to that part," Orphant Annie laughed. "You see there are many different kinds of creatures living in the big woods, and there are some who can not get along well with the others. Now where the little Gnome lived, there also lived another creature who did not like the little Gnome. This creature was a little old weazened-up man who was not much larger than the Gnome, but what he lacked in size, he made up in magic, for he had been given a large book, almost as large as himself. And this book was filled with magic prescriptions. The little old weazened-up man's name was Minky and the creatures of the woods called him Minky-the-Magician. Minky was as different from the little Gnome as day is from night, for while the little Gnome liked to help those who were in need of help, Minky did not like to help them at all. In fact, Minky-the-Magician did all that he could to keep the little Gnome from doing good!"

When Mrs. Bunnikin's rabbit babies ate bitter toadstools, the little Gnome
ran over to the Bunnikin home and gave them just the right kind of medicine,
so their fat little stomachs would not ache

"Dear me!" Bessie exclaimed, "I shouldn't like Minky at all!"

"Nor I either!" Carl chimed in.

Orphant Annie merely smiled as if there was much the two children had to learn, and continued her story. "Minky-the-Magician lived in a tree only a short distance from the oak in which the little Gnome lived, and while the little Gnome knew that Minky lived there, he had never seen him go in or out the door to his tree-home! And the reason that the little Gnome could not see Minky go in and out of the tree was because in the large book that Minky owned there was a very, very magical prescription which when taken three times a day would make whoever took it invisible. So you see that was why the little Gnome could not see Minky, though Minky could see the little Gnome very plainly and often followed him when he went through the woods to help some of his neighbors. And old weazened-up Minky-the-Magician became very angry and stamped his feet when he saw how the other creatures of the woods loved the little Gnome. For you surely must have guessed that Minky disliked any one to love another, if he disliked having any one do a generous deed. And it was all on account of his magic invisible potion. This potion is made out of very, very bitter roots and weeds, stewed for two nights the first of the month. The invisible potion is so very, very bitter it makes any one who takes it three times a day, wrinkle up his face so much that he finally gets so he wears wrinkles all the time, and gets to be just as peevish and disagreeable as he looks.

"You know everybody likes to see happy smiling faces even if he is sorrowful himself. That is, almost all people do. But Minky grew so ugly and disagreeable that he did not like to see any one happy. So he tried his utmost to keep the little Gnome from doing any kindly little deeds.

"Now there is one funny thing about the magic invisible potion that Minky-the-Magician made, and that is, while it made Minky invisible to those with eyes, it did not make him invisible to things without eyes!"

"Dear me!" Carl cried, "I don't see how that could be! For if things don't have eyes, then they can not possibly see!"

Orphant Annie laughed. "You are right, Carl, in what you say about seeing, but you will understand what I mean when I finish telling you the story.

"When Minky-the-Magician came anywhere near Freddy Fox or Mickie Mole or any of the other woodland creatures, they could not see him but they could scent him, and if Minky-the-Magician happened to be looking intently at something

when any of the woodland creatures came quietly along, they could bump right into him and knock him head over heels! So you see, even if Minky-the-Magician was invisible, he could be scented and he could be felt.

"One day Wally Woodpecker, the woodland mail carrier, who wears such a fine red hat, brought the little Gnome word that Mrs. Henrietta Hedgehog wanted him to run right over to her house, for one of the Hedgehog twins had swallowed an acorn and had a very bad stomach-ache. So the little Gnome picked up his medicine case and ran out the door of his tree-home as fast as he could run, and as it happened, Minky-the-Magician was at that moment looking through the little Gnome's keyhole, so when the little Gnome ran out through the door, he bumped right smack into Minky-the-Magician and knocked him down. The little Gnome was surprised to feel such a bump and not be able to see what caused it, but he was in a hurry, so, picking up his hat, he ran on through the woods to Mrs. Henrietta's home. Of course the little Gnome did not know that Minky-the-Magician was very angry because he had been bumped into and knocked over,

nor did he know that Minky had a large stick with which he intended whacking the little Gnome when he caught up with him. Nor did the little Gnome know that Minky-the-Magician was so close at his heels when he opened Mrs. Henrietta Hedgehog's door and slammed it shut behind him. If the little Gnome had known that Minky-the-Magi-

14

cian was so close to him, I am sure he would not have slammed the door, for you see Minky's nose was inside and the rest of him was outside, and although the door could not see him, still it held him fast.

"The little Gnome found that the Hedgehog twin had not swallowed an acorn, but was crying because he *wanted* to swallow an acorn and knew if he did it would make his little stomach ache. So with the little Hedgehog twin crying so loudly, no one heard Minky-the-Magician screaming because the door had slammed on his nose and held him fast. Finally when the little Gnome gave the Hedgehog twin a spoonful of honey and quieted him, they heard Minky-the-Magician kicking on the door and crying.

"Neither the little Gnome nor Mrs. Henrietta Hedgehog could imagine what was causing all the noise, so they ran and opened the door. Then Minky-the-Magician became so angry at them that his invisible medicine would not work and they saw him just as plainly as they saw each other.

"My! wasn't Minky-the-Magician hopping mad! He struck at the little Gnome with a big stick, but the little Gnome caught the stick and took it away from Minky. Then the little Gnome left Minky-the-Magician, and went back to his home. But Minky followed the little Gnome all the way home and as he went he told the little Gnome what he would do to him. 'I'll learn a charm that will change you into a monkey!' Minky cried. But the little Gnome pretended not to hear and when he reached his tree-house he went in and closed the door so that Minky could not follow.

"Then Minky-the-Magician went home and got out his large book to find a way to change the little Gnome into a monkey, but there was not a thing in the book about monkeys.

"Minky-the-Magician sat up all night reading his book and thinking of mean things to do to the little Gnome; and in the morning he had a long list.

15

"And Minky-the-Magician did all the things he planned to do to the little Gnome except change him into something else. This he could not do for, you know, when one's heart is filled with happiness and love, there is no room for anything else, and so one can not be changed at all. But Minky did a great many things to the little Gnome. He put burrs in his bed and stretched strings across his doorway so the little Gnome would trip and fall when he came out to take a walk. After a while, the little Gnome grew tired of having these tricks played on him, so he moved from the wood and came over here and made his home in the apple tree.

"And even then Minky-the-Magician followed him all the way here to play mean tricks on the little Gnome. But one day when Minky was away from home, Charlie Chipmunk, seeing Minky's door open, went inside and found the large book of magic. Now Charlie Chipmunk could not read but he knew that Harry Hootowl could, for Harry had gone to night school for a long, long time.

"So Charlie Chipmunk ran over to Harry Hootowl's home and brought Harry to Minky's house. There, Harry read in the book how to take wrinkles out of any one's face, and he would have read a lot more only Minky happened to come home and find them reading his book.

16

"Minky-the-Magician was angry at them and chased them from his house, but Harry Hootowl remembered what he had read and at the first opportunity he told the little Gnome. Then the little Gnome made up the magic potion to remove wrinkles and with the help of other woodland creatures, he caught Minky-the-Magician and scrubbed him all over with the magic potion to remove wrinkles.

"And the more they scrubbed, the more Minky-the-Magician wiggled and twisted and squirmed and giggled, and it was not until they had finished that they learned why Minky had been laughing all the time they were taking away his wrinkles, for, you see, as each wrinkle was washed away, it let a little happiness into Minky's heart, so that when they had finished, Minky-the-Magician sat on the ground and laughed and laughed until all the woodfolk came to see what was the cause of so much happiness.

"Then Minky-the-Magician caught hold of the little Gnome's hands and they danced all about the other creatures until they were tired.

"I tell you what, this made all the woodfolk very happy, and it made the little Gnome very happy too.

"Minky-the-Magician had completely changed from an old wrinkly, weazened-up person into a smooth-faced, smiling creature, and he invited every one into his great tree-home where he had a magic soda-water fountain.

"And Minky told them all that any time they wanted a drink of soda-water they could come right in and help themselves, 'For,' he said, 'I do not wish to live here any more and I will give the tree to all the woodland folk for a meeting place!'

"So the little Gnome asked Minky-the-Magician where he intended to live and Minky said that he would find a place somewhere. 'Why don't you come and live with me in the apple tree, Minky?'

"And Minky said he thought that would be very nice, so he moved right in with the little Gnome and the two of them have been living there for years and years. And do you know it is very hard to tell Minky from the little Gnome when you see them together. I do not believe that many of the woodfolk know whether it is Minky or the little Gnome who is doing kindnesses for them!"

"Does Minky-the-Magician help the little Gnome take care of the woodland creatures?" Bessie asked.

"Oh, yes!" Orphant Annie replied. "And he has taught the little Gnome all the good magic there was in the large magic book, so that between the two of them, they can do a great deal of good and bring a lot of happiness to the woodland creatures.

"Gracious me! Was that eleven o'clock that just struck?" Orphant Annie cried as she got to her feet. "I'll have to fry these potatoes in a jiffy for I heard your Daddy say he wanted an early dinner so he could get into town around one o'clock!"

And with this, Orphant Annie ran into the kitchen, leaving the children sitting on the porch step gazing in the direction of the gnarled apple tree, in the hope that they might catch a glimpse of the little Gnome or the Magician who had been changed from an ugly selfish creature into a happy one with a heart filled with sympathy and love for others.

III

THE GRANDPA-HORSE, THE RAG-MAN AND THE WHANGWHIZZLE

THE gentle old "family horse," Dan, wandered lazily up to the fence and stood with his nose resting on the top rail. Occasionally he swung his head around to his shoulder to frighten away a persistent fly, but unless the fly bit him, he made no motion, except a twitching of his hide or a lazy brush of his tail. He had been in the family long before Carl and Bessie were born, and now he spent his old age in contentedly eating his fill of clover during the summer and a meal of corn and oats every day in the winter.

Of course there had been a time when Dan was jumpy and frisky and would cut up all sorts of "didoes," dancing over the sidewalks when the band played, or some one suddenly raised an umbrella, or a trolley car passed by. But Dan had outgrown all that foolishness and although now and then he tried to be gay, he was usually too tired even to roll over.

As old Dan stood with his head resting on the top rail of the fence, Orphant Annie walked out and gave him some sugar to eat. While she was talking to him and rubbing his soft nose, Carl and Bessie came around the house and joined her.

When Orphant Annie had given old Dan the last lump of sugar, she and the children sat down on the grass and gazed up at the tired old horse. There was a twinkle in Orphant Annie's eyes as she nodded her head and said: "Dan, I believe you were fibbing to me!" Carl and Bessie smiled, but remained silent. "If you two could understand horse talk, I'd have old Dan tell you what he just told me!" laughed Orphant Annie as she lay back on the grass and pillowed her head upon her arms. "But you can't understand him so I'll tell you myself what it was.

"He said that his great-great-grandfather-horse worked for a man who did nothing but pick up rags and bottles and bones and pieces of iron and brass which he sold to a junk dealer. And he said that the rag-man for whom he worked was such a gentle and kindly man that he never touched him with a whip or even spoke crossly to him. Every evening Dan's grandpa-horse and the rag-man went to the rag-man's home and the rag-man always fed and watered the grandpa-horse before he ate his own supper. And the rag-man was very, very poor for he only made a few pennies each day. But all the children in the town liked the rag-man and his grandpa-horse, because the rag-man gave them pennies to buy goodies with, and the old grandpa-horse would let them climb all over his back or even pull his tail without so much as flicking an ear.

"But there were people in the town who did not like the rag-man. It may have been because he was just a rag-man, or it may have been because he was poor and did not live in a fine house and wear fine clothes as they did. Anyway, one of the persons who did not like the rag-man and the grandpa-horse was a very rich man with very fine clothes, who had lots and lots of gold dollars and who owned lots and lots of big houses. In fact, he even owned the barn in which the rag-man and his grandpa-horse lived. But the rich man would never do anything for any of his houses. He let them go until the roofs leaked and the people had to sit in bed with

One day when the rag-man was scratching in a trash pile, he picked up a
queer little box

umbrellas up when it rained real hard. So of course very few people liked the selfish rich man. But the rag-man never complained to the rich man about the barn. Instead, when he got home at night, he often went to work to nail boards up where they had fallen down and to do what he could to fix up the place.

"One day when the rag-man was scratching in a trash pile, he picked up a queer little box. It was a little black box only two inches long and an inch wide, and it had little hinges on it. The kindly old rag-man always talked to the grandpa-horse, so now he held up the queer little black box and said, 'What do you suppose this funny little box was made for?' And the old grandpa-horse, because he didn't know the answer, just kept still. So the rag-man put the box in his pocket and went on scratching in the trash pile. When he had all the pieces of rags and iron he could find, he took them to the junk dealer's place and received ten pennies for them. Then he and the old grandpa-horse started home. But on the way to their home, they met ten little boys who looked as if they needed something to eat, so the kindly old rag-man gave them each a penny with which to buy a bun.

"Then when they reached their home, the rag-man fed and watered the old grandpa-horse, and went into his own part of the barn and ate his supper. And when he had finished his supper, the rag-man took the queer little black box from his pocket and looked at it, then he shook it and something inside rattled.

"The old grandpa-horse could see and hear all this through the window; he even saw the rag-man take out his knife and pry up the lid on its rusty hinges.

"When the lid of the queer little black box came up, what do you suppose was inside? Well, you would never guess," said Orphant Annie, "for *I* tried to guess when old Dan was telling me the story and I had to give up! It was a Whang-

whizzle. Now I thought at first that a Whangwhizzle was
some kind of fireworks, like a Snake-in-the-Grass which ex-
plodes with a loud pop when it gets through fizzling and
chasing about, but it isn't that at all. A Whangwhizzle is a
little teeny, weeny wrinkled-up Elf, and this one said he had
been shut up in the box for years and years, just like the
Genii the fisherman found in the bottle. Don't you remember?
The Whangwhizzle was only an inch and a half high, but
being even that small, he did not have very much room in
the little box and if it hadn't been for his magic, he probably
would have been very hungry. But the Whangwhizzle seemed
mighty glad to be out in the air once again, for in his joy
he jumped over a teacup and danced about the rag-man's
table, kicking up his tiny heels and making little squeaky
noises like a mouse.

23

"The Whangwhizzle was the cutest little creature the rag-man had ever seen and he smiled as he watched the little fellow jump about and squeak in his happiness. Finally when the Whangwhizzle had danced enough, he perched himself on the edge of the rag-man's cup and said, 'Thank you so much for getting me out of that box! I will let you make any wish you want to make and it will come true! You can have all the money you wish, or anything you like!'

"Now when he was a boy the rag-man had read a story about a man and his wife who had been given three wishes and the wife wished for a chain of sausages, and this foolish wish made her husband so peevish, he wished that the sausages were hanging on her nose. Then there was only one wish left and that was to wish the sausages off the wife's nose, so when they got through, the foolish couple did not have anything more than they had before they wished. So the rag-man said to the Whangwhizzle, 'I do not wish to be paid for

releasing you from the queer little black box, for I have my reward in knowing that your freedom has given you happiness.'

"Then the Whangwhizzle took off his little hat and scratched his head in a puzzled manner, 'Jimminycrickets!' he squeaked. 'You are the first person I have ever met who did not wish for nearly everything!'

" 'Well!' the rag-man replied. 'You see I have a very dear old friend looking through the window there, and we go about our business every day and see all sorts of people. Some are rich and some are poor, but we have found that happiness does not mean having wealth, nor does it mean having many servants, for we find that those who have the least are sometimes the happiest!'

"The Whangwhizzle put on his little hat, jumped off the rag-man's cup, walked across the table and held out his teeny, weeny hand for the rag-man to shake. And the rag-man with a happy laugh took the Whangwhizzle's teeny, weeny hand between his thumb and finger and shook it.

" 'Thank you just the same!' he said to the Whangwhizzle. 'But I do not care to wish for anything!'

"Then the Whangwhizzle winked at the rag-man and said, 'Then put me back in the queer little black box and lose the box along the street somewhere, for I have been giving wishes to people for opening the box for hundreds of years and you are the first one who did not wish for something foolish! And when you have put me in the box and lost me, you will find that I have given you something that you have not needed but which is the greatest gift a man can have!' So the rag-man put the little teeny, weeny Whangwhizzle back in the box, and the next day lost it along the road somewhere. And the rag-man and the old grandpa-horse went about the town picking up bits of rags and bottles and pieces of iron to sell to the junk dealer for a few pennies each day just as they had done before, and the little children liked the rag-man and played with the grandpa-horse; and the mamas and daddies of the children liked the rag-man, too, because he was generous and kindly to every creature. Even the rich man and the others in the town who had not liked the rag-man and his grandpa-horse before, now nodded pleasantly to him as he passed!"

Orphant Annie stopped, and after waiting a moment to see if she would continue, the children both asked, "But Orphant Annie, what was it that the Whangwhizzle gave the rag-man that he did not need?"

"Well, sir!" Orphant Annie laughed, "that was just what I asked old Dan here, when you came around the house, but he was so sleepy, I guess he forgot what his great-great-grandpa-horse told him the Whangwhizzle gave the rag-man. And I don't know any way to find out unless old Dan will tell us now!"

"What was it, Dan?" the children asked.

The old "family horse" raised one ear slightly at the sound of his name, whisked his tail lazily over his back, but did not open his eyes.

"You see!" laughed Orphant Annie as she shook her finger at the tired old horse, "I said he didn't know himself, and I wouldn't be surprised if he made the whole story up as he went along!"

IV

GERTRUDE GARTERSNAKE AND THE THREE GOBLINS

ONE day Orphant Annie drove old Dobbin to town to do some marketing and of course the children went with her. Old Dobbin, you know, was old Dan's younger brother. As they turned into the lane leading to the house a little snake wiggled across the path just in time for old Dobbin to step on it. Orphant Annie gave the reins a jerk but was too late to save the little creature. She and the children climbed out of the buggy and looked at the snake. It was one of the prettily colored, harmless kind, commonly known as a Garter snake.

"Poor little thing!" said Orphant Annie. "Maybe it was on its way to the grocery store for its Mama!"

"Its tail is still wiggling!" Carl said. "It'll keep wiggling till sundown. That's what the Hired Man says!"

"That isn't the reason its tail wiggles!" said Orphant Annie as she climbed into the buggy again and smacked the reins on Dobbin's back.

"You know Goblins are full of fun and mischief," said Orphant Annie.

"Yes!" the children answered, although they did not know what this had to do with snakes' tails wiggling.

"Well!" said Orphant Annie, "there were three little Goblins who lived in a little mud house upon the bank of a little green river—Gooby Goblin, Gibby Goblin and Gobby Goblin. They were brothers and though queer-looking creatures with large eyes and ears, still they were rather cute on account of being so small. They wore——"

"How small were they, Orphant Annie?" Carl asked.

"About ten inches high," Orphant Annie replied. "And they wore little pointed hats and little pointed pants and little pointed coats and they had eyebrows that stuck up from their heads just like pictures you see of Goblins. Gooby Goblin and Gibby Goblin and Gobby Goblin lived in the cunning little mud house and Gertrude Gartersnake kept the place clean and cooked their dinners for them!"

"Did Gertrude Gartersnake sweep the floors for them?" Carl wished to know.

"Certainly!" Orphant Annie replied.

"Haw! Haw! Haw!" Carl laughed. "How could she sweep the floors when she didn't have any hands?"

Orphant Annie pulled up on the reins and stopped the horse as if to emphasize what she was about to say. "The little Goblins made a little flat brush," said Orphant Annie, "with two pieces of tape upon the top. So when Gertrude Gartersnake wished to sweep the floor, as she did every day, she crawled part of the way through the two loops of tape and then wiggled about the room until it was nice and clean. Now if you ask me any more questions about how she did things, I shan't tell you!" Orphant Annie laughed. "You have to guess some of them yourselves!

"Well, anyway," she went on, "the three little Goblins,

Gooby, Gibby and Gobby, often played pranks upon others and if they were caught, they sometimes had their ears boxed. And that is not very pleasant. So when the three little Goblins started out to play a prank on any one they always said to Gertrude Gartersnake, 'Now if Old Mister Doodlesnipper, or any one else comes to the house and says he will wait until we return, you must put your tail out through a crack in the door and wiggle it. So if we see your tail wiggling, we'll know he's here and we won't come in until he leaves!' And Gertrude Gartersnake promised she would do this.

"But, you know, Gooby and Gibby and Gobby Goblin played so many pranks upon so many people and there were so many folks waiting at the queer little mud house to spank the Goblins or box their ears, that Gertrude Gartersnake spent most of her time wiggling her tail out the chink in the door, for she did not know when the Goblins might return and be caught.

"So one day when the three little Goblins had played a prank on Old Mister Doodlesnipper and had almost been caught, Old Mister Doodlesnipper said to himself, 'I'll just go to their house and wait until they come home and then I'll *lambaste* them!' And he took his knife and cut three switches; one for Gooby Goblin, one for Gibby Goblin and one for Gobby Goblin; and then he walked down to the Goblins' queer little mud house. In he walked without knocking and found Gertrude Gartersnake frying pancakes for the Goblins' supper.

"When Gertrude Gartersnake saw Old Mister Doodlesnipper with three switches, she thought, 'Now he's come to *lambaste* them.' So she quit frying the pancakes and put her tail out the front door and began to wiggle it.

"Old Mister Doodlesnipper wasn't such a foolish old man as you might think from his name!" said Orphant Annie. "So he put on his specks and rubbed his nose. 'Now!' he said to

Old Mister Doodlesnipper didn't say a word, he just went out to the kitchen and ate all the Goblins' pancakes and maple syrup and then came in and sat down facing Gertrude Gartersnake

himself, 'Gertrude Gartersnake was busy frying pancakes when I walked in, and when she saw me so mad and with these switches, she wiggles to the front door and puts her tail out! This is about the fifth time I have been here to catch them Goblins and each time she has done that!'

"So Old Mister Doodlesnipper went out in the kitchen and pretended he was going to get a drink, but instead he slipped around and peeped about the front of the house. Old Mister Doodlesnipper had to laugh in spite of himself as he walked back into the Goblins' house, for Gertrude Gartersnake's tail was out the front door wiggling like a flag-man trying to stop a train. Old Mister Doodlesnipper didn't say a word, he just went out to the kitchen and ate all the Goblins' pancakes and maple syrup and then came in the front room and sat down facing Gertrude Gartersnake. When it began to get dark, Gertrude Gartersnake said, 'Mister Doodlesnipper, ahem, did I hear your wife calling you?' And Old Mister Doodlesnipper said, 'No, Gertrude Gartersnake, you didn't hear my wife calling me! 'Cause why? 'Cause I hain't got no wife!'

31

"And it grew later and later and the dew fell on the grass and Gertrude Gartersnake thought, 'Poor Gooby and Gibby and Gobby Goblin, you'll be all wet and drippy with the dew, and I'll bet you'll be hungry! I wish Old Mister Doodlesnipper would go home!' Then she thought and thought while she wiggled her tail out the door and finally she said, 'Mister Doodlesnipper, did I hear your Mama calling you?' And Old Mister Doodlesnipper said, 'No, Gertrude Gartersnake, you didn't hear my Mammy calling me! 'Cause why? 'Cause I hain't got no Mammy!' Then Old Mister Doodlesnipper pulled another chair up and put his feet in it and went to sleep, but Gertrude Gartersnake kept her tail out the front door and wiggled it all night for she did not know when the three little Goblins might return. Of course Gertrude Gartersnake did not know that Gooby and Gibby and Gobby Goblin had crawled into a woodchuck hole and had gone to sleep. If she had known this, Gertrude Gartersnake could have saved her tail from being almost wiggled off. But she did not know it, so she kept her promise and wiggled her tail until morning. Then she was so tired she fell asleep.

"So when Gibby and Gooby and Gobby came home and did not see Gertrude Gartersnake's tail sticking out the door and wiggling, they thought Old Mister Doodlesnipper had gone home. So into the house they walked and slammed the kitchen door behind them. This awakened Old Mister Doodlesnipper and he *lambasted* the three little Goblins until his switches were all worn out. Then he went home after promising the Goblins he would give them more the next time.

"Gooby and Gibby and Gobby Goblin were very angry at first with Gertrude Gartersnake, but when she told them how she had wiggled her tail out the front door all night, they forgave her. 'But,' they said, 'it will not do for us to get caught this way again; we will fix your tail so that it will wiggle even if you get killed.' So they made a magic liquid and put it on Gertrude Gartersnake's tail, and after that even if Gertrude went to sleep her tail would keep on wiggling. And Gertrude Gartersnake took some of the magic liquid and gave it to all the other snakes; and that is why all snakes' tails wiggle even after they have been killed," said Orphant Annie, as she stopped old Dobbin by the side door and started to carry the bundles into the house.

V

WHY THE LADYBUG IS RED

"HELLO there, little Lizzy Ladybug!" Orphant Annie cried, as she held up her hand upon which a ladybug had just alighted.

Carl and Bessie drew close to Orphant Annie and watched the tiny little creature fold its wrinkly brown wings up under their red cap-shaped coverings. Then they all laughed when Orphant Annie said, "No, it isn't Lizzy Ladybug after all! At first I thought it was!"

"How can you tell, Orphant Annie?" Carl asked.

"It's easy!" Orphant Annie replied. "See, it is Larry Ladybug! You can tell him because his shirt-tail is sticking out!" Orphant Annie showed the children the little brown wrinkly wings which the Ladybug had not drawn completely under the cup-like coverings. When Larry Ladybug had washed his little eyebrows with his front feet, he began to walk toward the highest part of Orphant Annie's hand. "Now watch!" whispered Orphant Annie, "and you will see just how foolish little Ladybugs are!" And sure enough when Larry Ladybug reached the top of Orphant Annie's hand she turned her hand over so that the Ladybug was underneath.

34

The Ladybugs had a very cunning teeny weeny house made out of an acorn,
with three little windows and a cute little door

"See!" laughed Orphant Annie, "he will climb to the top every time, no matter how often you turn your hand!"

"Why does he do that?" Bessie wondered.

"Because he doesn't know any better!" laughed Orphant Annie. "He thinks he has traveled a long, long way, I guess, and he is still right where he started from! Just like a whole lot of people!" Orphant Annie added.

"Are all Ladybugs just as foolish?" Carl asked.

"Nearly all of them are!" Orphant Annie said. "That's how they happened to get painted red!"

"Oh, Orphant Annie!" Bessie cried, "Ladybugs grow that way, they are not painted!"

"Maybe Orphant Annie knows what she's talking about," Carl told Bessie.

"Ladybugs are all this color now," Orphant Annie said very seriously. "But there was a time when they were white! Just as white as a snow-flake!"

"When was that, Orphant Annie?" both children cried in one breath.

"Oh, it was a long, long time ago, and just as soon as I look in the oven at the roast, I'll tell you how it all happened." And with this, Orphant Annie, with the Ladybug still walking around and around her hand, went into the kitchen.

ORPHANT ANNIE

Presently Orphant Annie came out and sat on the porch steps between the children and as she talked the little Ladybug continued to circle her hand while the children watched it intently.

"Yes, siree bob! The Ladybugs were as white as snow and they lived together under a bush that was out in the woods. They had a very cunning teeny weeny house made out of an acorn, with three little windows and a cute little door. There was a chimney, too, and inside were two rooms, a kitchen and a living-room. The living-room was the Lady-bugs' parlor in the daytime and their bedroom at night; for they had a folding couch which was very soft and fluffy when made into a bed, and was red and plushy in the daytime. Those were the first two ladybugs that ever lived; they were the Mama Ladybug and the Daddy Ladybug. Mama Lady-bug went visiting quite often after she had swept up the breakfast crumbs and made the bed into a red plushy couch. And Daddy Ladybug walked out of the house and down the little weeny bug path that led to the little bug village. Daddy Ladybug carried his lunch every day, that he might not have to come home until evening. So, you see, that left quite a lot of time for Mama Ladybug to call on her neighbors and attend to the shopping before Daddy Ladybug came home.

"Well, sir! One day Mama Ladybug had watched Daddy Ladybug go out of the teeny weeny front door of the acorn house and walk down the little path until he disappeared from her sight, about three or four feet away.

"Then Mama Ladybug put on her little black bonnet and started down to the Grasshopper grocery to get a few seeds to bake the next day. As she walked along singing a Ladybug song, Mama Ladybug came to Aunty Katydid's house!"

"What kind of a house did the Katykid have?" Carl wanted to know.

"Well," Orphant Annie laughed, "Aunty Katydid, being

quite a mite larger than Mama Ladybug, had a larger house, and it was made of a corncob all whittled out nice and smooth inside, with two doors, one at each end. Aunty Katydid's house was not nearly so cunning as Mama Ladybug's house, for it did not have any windows, nor any chimney and it only had one long room, like a hall. But, do you know, every time Daddy Ladybug walked by Aunty Katydid's corncob house, he sighed and said, 'Wish I had a long house to live in,' and every time Mama Ladybug went to the Grasshopper grocery and stopped in to see Aunty Katydid, she said to herself, 'Wish I had a long house like this to live in.' And on this morning, when she stopped to visit with Aunty Katydid, Mama Ladybug said out loud, 'Wish I had a long house like this to live in.' And Aunty Katydid replied, 'Land sakes, Mama Ladybug, you can have it and welcome too, for I'm just getting ready to move!'

" 'Where you movin' to?' asked Mama Ladybug.

" 'I'm movin' over to Hoptoad Lane in a brand-new corn-cob with red floors!'

" 'Land sakes!' cried Mama Ladybug. 'Then I guess I'll move right in when you move out, Aunty Katydid!'

" 'All rightee!' said Aunty Katydid. 'I'm all out but these few chairs and Charlie Cricket will be along pretty soon with his caterpillar pony to take them. It's the last load!'

" 'Suppose I could get him to move me?' asked Mama Ladybug.

" 'Wouldn't surprise me a mite, but if he can't get back until late this evening, what then, Mama Ladybug?'

" 'Then I suppose I'll have to wait until he does get back.'

"Just then the two friends heard Charlie Cricket's little wagon wheels go 'wheekity wheekity' and they looked out the front door and there he was driving right up the path to the Katydid's corncob house.

"Mama Ladybug asked Charlie Cricket if he would move

Just then the two friends heard Charlie Cricket's little wagon wheels go "wheekity wheekity" and they looked out the front door and there he was driving right up the path to the Katydid's corncob house

her things out of the cunning little acorn house. And Charlie Cricket said 'deed, he would be glad to when he got back from Aunty Katydid's new corncob house.

. "So Mama Ladybug promised Aunty Katydid that she would come over and see her some day and asked Aunty Katydid to come back and see her too.

"Then after Aunty Katydid had gone, Mama Ladybug sat down and thought, 'I believe I'll run down to town and tell Daddy Ladybug. He'll be mighty tickled I know!'

"So Mama Ladybug ran all the way down to the little bug village and told Daddy Ladybug. And Daddy Ladybug was real tickled.

"'I'll tell you what, Mama Ladybug!' Daddy Ladybug said, 'you go back home and pack all the dishes, and I'll bring a lot of paint and we'll paint the inside of the corncob house just like Aunty Katydid's new house!'

"Mama Ladybug thought this was very nice, so she ran home to pack the dishes and Daddy Ladybug took a lot of paint and painted the long hall of the new corncob house. Then when Charlie Cricket did not return from Aunty Katydid's house and it began to grow dark, instead of staying in their own cozy, cunning little acorn house until morning, Daddy Ladybug ran over and said, 'Mama Ladybug, shall we spend the night at the new house?' And Mama Ladybug said, 'You betcha!' and hippitty hop they went right over in the dark to their corncob house. But the paint was still wet and the two foolish Ladybugs had to crawl up to the ceiling of the long corncob hall and hang there all night."

"I would rather have stayed in the cunning little acorn house," said Bessie.

"So would I," exclaimed Carl.

"Well, that's just what I say!" Orphant Annie agreed, as she smiled at the Ladybug still walking up her hand. "But they went anyway and climbed to the top of the hallway out

of the wet paint. Then they had hardly got to sleep when some larger creature, running through the woods, stepped on the corncob house and sent it rolling down the hill. And as the corncob house went rolling along, Mama and Daddy Ladybug began running around the sides of the long hallway, first across the ceiling, then as the corncob turned over, they found themselves running across the wet paint. And when their feet got covered with the wet paint, they would slip from the ceiling and, splash! they would fall down into the wet red paint upon their backs!"

Carl and Bessie joined in Orphant Annie's laughter as they thought of the two Ladybugs scrambling over the walls as the corncob house rolled along.

"Finally," said Orphant Annie, "when the corncob house stopped rolling, Mama Ladybug and Daddy Ladybug were so tired they just lay down where they were and went sound asleep. And in the morning, what a sight they were! Their backs were covered with red paint that had dried hard in the night, so instead of being nice white Ladybugs, they were red Ladybugs.

"Mama Ladybug looked at Daddy Ladybug and cried and cried, and Daddy Ladybug looked at Mama Ladybug and he cried and cried. At last, thinking of their nice little cozy acorn house, they opened the door of the corncob house and there right before them they saw their own little acorn house. The corncob house had rolled straight down the hill and had stopped just in front of their old home.

"Mama and Daddy Ladybug hurried inside the acorn house and put some water on to heat, so that they might wash off the red paint, but no matter how hard they scrubbed, only a few little spots of the paint would come off and as these spots turned black they decided to remain as they were. And," Orphant Annie said, as she gave a puff that blew the little Ladybug off her hand, high in the air, "they have always been red with the little black spots ever since. And when their children came, why, the children were red with black spots, too!"

"And I suppose, running around the corncob house that night is what makes them always run to the top of everything, just like this Ladybug did on your hand!" Carl laughed.

"I suppose that is the reason!" Orphant Annie said, as she rose and went into the kitchen to see if the roast was done.

VI

THE NINE LITTLE GOBLINS WITH GREEN EYES

"ONCE there were nine little goblins with green eyes!" said Orphant Annie, when the children had teased her into telling them a story. "And they had nine little goblin wives with red eyes. The nine little goblin wives had red eyes because they spent all their time in weeping. They were always sad, it seemed, and nothing the nine little green-eyed goblins could do seemed to please them.

"If it happened to be a rainy day, one of the little green-eyed goblins would look out of the window and say: 'Ho, ho! It's raining to-day!' And at that all of the nine little goblin wives would begin crying in different keys, which sounded so funny that the nine little green-eyed goblin husbands would have to run out in the kitchen and snicker with their hankies in their mouths to keep their wives from hearing them laugh. For the nine little green-eyed goblins were happy little fellows and could see fun in almost anything.

"And when the goblins awakened in the morning to find the sun shining brightly, if one of the little green-eyed goblins

43

looked out of the window and said, 'Ho, ho! It's going to be a wonderful day!' all the nine little red-eyed goblin wives would start crying in their different keys. For, you see, it made no difference whether it was clear or cloudy, everything seemed wrong to the little red-eyed goblin wives.

"Well, sir," Orphant Annie exclaimed, "the nine little goblins with green eyes lived with their nine little goblin wives with red eyes for nine hundred years and always the little goblin wives were sad and teary, until finally the little green-eyed goblins could stand it no longer and went out behind the goblin barn where they kept their goblin ponies and had a long talk. After they had talked it all over for two hours, the nine little goblins decided there was nothing to do except go out into the world and find some remedy to drive away their wives' sadness. So they all went inside the house and packed their valises and kissed their little red-eyed goblin wives good-by. Then they hopped upon their nine little goblin ponies and with the howls of their nine little red-eyed goblin wives ringing in their goblin ears, they flew away through the world to find something to make their wives laugh.

"When the nine little goblins with the green eyes came to the end of the road, at the place where there was nothing beyond except a great deep canyon, they stopped and one little goblin said, 'Now let us search until we find something very, very funny and at the close of a year we will meet here at the end of the road and will go home together!' All the other little goblins agreed to this and they shook hands and flew their little goblin ponies out over the canyon and up into the air, each taking the direction he thought best.

"At the close of the year the nine little goblins again met at the end of the road and each had a present for his wife. So they all shook hands and said 'Hello!' and galloped their little goblin ponies home as fast as they could go. When they

44

reached home, the nine little goblin wives with red eyes were sitting in the parlor crying and when the nine little goblins with green eyes walked in, the nine little goblin wives cried: 'Where in the world have you been?' And they were so glad to see their nine little green-eyed goblin husbands they all began to sob.

"The nine little goblins with green eyes looked at one another and blinked their eyes, for they could not understand why any one should be so happy he would cry and howl about it. But they didn't say anything, they just sat down on the floor and began unwrapping the presents they had brought their little red-eyed goblin wives.

"The first one unwrapped a queer little box and handed it to his little red-eyed goblin wife at which she and the other little red-eyed wives quit their crying. 'Unwrap it!' said the little green-eyed goblin. So all were quiet and still while the little goblin's red-eyed wife unfastened the queer little box. And when the little red-eyed goblin wife slipped the catch to the queer little box the lid flew open and a jack-in-the-box jumped up and hit her on the nose. At this the nine little goblins with green eyes rolled over and over on the floor and kicked up their little goblin heels and laughed and laughed. But the nine little goblin wives with red eyes began to cry and they cried and cried in different keys until another little goblin with green eyes opened his package.

"And that is the way it went until all the presents were opened. One little goblin brought a parrot with red and yellow and blue feathers which sang ridiculous songs in a very funny tone of voice. And the parrot's songs made the nine little goblins with green eyes roll over with laughter, but the nine red-eyed goblin wives only cried and sobbed.

"Each time a present was unwrapped, the nine little goblins with green eyes thought it was very, very funny and the nine little red-eyed goblin wives thought it was very, very sad.

The nine little Goblins with green eyes flew their little goblin ponies out over the canyon and up into the air, each taking the direction he thought best

"So the nine little goblins with green eyes said to one another: 'It's no use! Nothing can cure them, they are unhappy unless they are unhappy. Perhaps we will make them happier by making them unhappier!'

"So they went out behind the goblin barn and whispered to one another. Then the next morning the nine little goblins with green eyes pretended they were still asleep until one of the wives looked out the window and saw that it was raining.

'Oh dear! It's raining!' she said and she burst into tears. Whereupon the other little goblin wives with red eyes immediately burst into tears, also. Then the nine little goblins with green eyes asked, 'Whasmatter?' in sleepy goblin voices. 'It's r-r-raining!' answered the nine little red-eyed goblin wives as they sobbed and sobbed.

" 'Dear me!' cried the nine little goblins with green eyes, 'It's raining!' and immediately they burst into sobs, and they sobbed and sobbed, and the goblin wives sobbed and sobbed, and all they did the live-long day was sob, sob, sob.

"And the next morning, very early one of the little red-eyed goblin wives looked out of the window and saw the sun shining brightly. 'Oh, dear!' she cried. 'The sun is shining!' and immediately she and all the other little red-eyed goblin wives burst into sobs.

"And when they told the nine little goblins with green eyes what was the trouble, the nine little goblins with green eyes immediately burst into sobs, too. So they all sobbed and sobbed and sobbed the live-long day.

"After supper the nine little goblins with green eyes winked at one another and began crying as loudly as they knew how, and they cried all night so that their nine little goblin wives with the red eyes could not sleep a wink. And at breakfast, instead of eating, the nine little goblins with green eyes sat down on the floor and howled and howled as if their little goblin hearts would break, while their nine little goblin wives with the red eyes ate their breakfast in silence and could not understand it at all.

"So the nine little goblins with green eyes howled all day and all the next night, making so much fuss with their howling that their nine little goblin wives with the red eyes had to go out in the kitchen and stuff their hankies in their ears. And so for six days the nine little goblins with the green eyes cried and howled at everything, stopping hardly long enough to get a drink of water. All this time their wives were so astonished they forgot to be sad. Then when the nine little goblins with green eyes thought they had howled enough, they suddenly quit.

"And their nine little goblin wives with the red eyes came and put their arms around them and said, 'You don't know what a relief it is to have you quit that silly, foolish howling over nothing! If we had not loved you so much, we would have taken the brooms to your little goblin backs!'

"Then the nine little goblins with green eyes winked at one another over their wives' shoulders and said: 'We will promise not to howl and blubber over trifles after this!'

"And their wives answered, 'That's nice, for you can't imagine how foolish it is to hear you all crying in different keys when there is nothing in the wide world to cry about.'

JOHNNY GRUELLE

"After that, the nine little goblins with green eyes and their nine little wives lived together in the happiest and pleasantest way, for none of them ever cried or howled about anything. And in a very short time the nine little goblin wives with the red eyes changed to nine little goblin wives with green eyes, for you know," said Orphant Annie, "it is crying that makes your eyes the reddest, and if you do not cry at all, your eyes always take on their natural color, and the natural color of all happy goblins' eyes is bright twinkly green. And that is the story of the nine little goblins with the green eyes."

"Didn't their wives ever find out the joke played on them, Orphant Annie?" Bessie asked.

"Oh, yes!" Orphant Annie replied. "And when the nine little goblins told their nine little goblin wives, the wives laughed as heartily as the husbands, for you see they had forgotten how to cry, long before that."

VII

THE GNOME IN THE PEANUT

WHEN the Hired Man returned from town he brought the children—Carl, Bessie and Orphant Annie—three bags of peanuts. After thanking the Hired Man, they raced out into the orchard and sat beneath the trees and ate the peanuts.

"Once there was a little weazened-up Gnome who lived on the top of a high hill," said Orphant Annie. "He was a stingy little Gnome too and lived all by himself. Whenever he saw any one coming up the hill to his house, the weazened-up little Gnome would run and hide, for fear that the visitor wished to borrow something. So one day, when the little Gnome saw a tall, strange-looking man walking up the hill to his home, he thought to himself, 'Now who is this, and what does he want? I guess he wants to beg something to eat.' And with that selfish thought in his heart, the little Gnome ran to his garden and hid beneath the vines until the tall, strange-looking man had gone. The next day the tall, strange-looking man came again, and again the little stingy

51

Gnome ran and hid in the garden beneath the vines until the man had gone. Now the little Gnome did not know it, but the tall, strange-looking man was a Magician and he had come to give the little Gnome something the little Gnome had lost years and years before.

"So, after the second time when he climbed the hill to the little Gnome's house, the Magician thought to himself: 'It's funny that the little Gnome is always away from home when I go there. I'll run down to this first house and ask his neighbor when is the best time to find him at home!'

"So the Magician went to the neighbor's house and knocked on the door, and a little boy and a little girl came to the door and said, 'Good morning!'

" 'Good morning!' said the Magician, as he patted both their curly heads. 'Do you know when is the best time to find the little Gnome at home?'

" 'Oh, yes sir,' the two children answered. 'You can find him at home always, because he never, never leaves the top of the hill.'

" 'But I was just up there,' said the Magician, 'and he was not at home.'

"The little boy and the little girl laughed. 'Oh, he was at home all right, but probably he thought you wished to borrow something and he ran and hid. He is very, very stingy,' they said.

" 'Then,' said the Magician, 'I will fool him,' and he gave each of the children a golden penny and went away.

"The next day, he climbed a tree from which he could look over the Gnome's hill and there he saw the little Gnome working about the house. As the Magician watched, he saw an old woman climbing the hill and as soon as the little Gnome saw a visitor coming, he ran to his garden and hid beneath the vines. So after climbing the long hill, the poor old woman had to leave without seeing the little Gnome.

"Then the Magician climbed down from the tree and went to the foot of the hill and met the poor old woman, and seeing that she was weeping, he asked: 'Why are you crying, Grandmother?'

" 'Because we have no bread in the house and my husband is ill in bed. I just walked up to the Gnome's house to borrow some, but he is never at home when a person wants to borrow anything.'

" 'Well, well, well, Grandmother,' the Magician said. 'Dry your eyes, for if it is something to eat that you wish, I can easily give you that,' and he went behind some bushes and pulled a little round box out of his belt and from the box he took a little round white pebble (it was the thing he was returning to the little Gnome). The Magician rubbed the little round white pebble once crossways and twice crisscrossways and said: 'Hokus, pokus! Let there be a basket of nice food and drink for this good old Granny!' and before you could say 'Jack Robinson,' there was the basket filled with food and drink upon the ground before him.

"The Magician carried the basket to the old woman and she was very, very grateful. 'If I owned the nice farm of the little Gnome,' the old woman said, 'I would soon be rich enough to repay you for this kindness!'

"'Oh, please do not thank me, Grandmother. I am very happy to be able to give you the food and drink. And all that I ask in return is that to-morrow at this time you meet me here again.'

"So the little old woman promised the Magician she would meet him at the foot of the little Gnome's hill the next day, and sure enough the Magician found her there when he came.

"'Now,' said the Magician, 'I wish you to climb the hill to the Gnome's house again and call for him when you get to the door, then you must sit on his front steps and wait until I come.'

"'All right,' the little old woman replied, and she started up the hill.

"Then the Magician ran and climbed the tree again so that he might watch the little Gnome, and as he watched he saw the little Gnome run and hide again under the vines in the garden.

"So the Magician climbed down from the tree and walked up the hill to the little Gnome's house where he found the little old woman waiting for him on the steps. 'Did you see the little Gnome, Grandmother?' the Magician asked.

"The little old woman smiled. 'No, indeed,' she replied, 'nor do any of the neighbors ever see him when they call up here, for he is so stingy he is afraid they are coming to borrow something and he runs and hides.'

"'I know that,' said the Magician, 'for I watched him hide from you yesterday and I watched him hide from you to-day.' And he told the little old woman how he had climbed the tree and watched.

"Then the Magician and the little old woman walked to the back of the house and called, 'Hey, little Gnome!' But everything was quiet.

"Then they called again, 'Ho, little Gnome!' But still everything was quiet. Then the Magician and the little old

"Oh, please do not thank me, Grandmother," said the Magician

woman walked to the edge of the garden and called again, 'Hi, little Gnome!' But the little Gnome still remained hidden amongst the vines.

"Then the Magician called once more, 'Ho, little Gnome! If you ever want to come out of the garden, you must come before I count three!'

"And the Magician counted three, but still the little weazened-up Gnome remained hidden in the vines.

"So the Magician took the little round box from his belt and the little white pebble from the little round box and he rubbed the pebble once crossways and twice crisscrossways and said, 'Hokus, pokus! May the little Gnome remain forever hidden amongst the vines!'

"Then the Magician turned to the little old woman and said: 'Is your husband well enough to climb this hill?'

"And the little old woman answered: 'Oh, dear no. He is so old and feeble he can scarcely raise his head!'

" 'Then, Grandmother, you must wait here until I go and fetch him.'

"So the Magician walked down the hill to the little old woman's shanty and inside on the bed he found an old man. 'Hello, Granddaddy!' said the Magician in his cheeriest tones. 'How do you feel to-day?'

"And the little old man smiled a sad smile and answered: 'I feel a little stronger to-day, thank you.'

"So the Magician laughed and said: 'I have some medicine here which will make you feel like a youngster again!' and he poured some of the medicine into a glass half-filled with water and held it to the old man's lips. And when the little old man had finished drinking the medicine, he looked strangely at the Magician and then at his own hands. Then he felt his arms with his hands, and his eyes stuck out with wonder, for the Magician's medicine was magic medicine and it had made the rittle old man young again.

" 'Now how do you feel?' asked the Magician.

"The man laughed and kicked the covers from the bed. 'Just as you said that I would,' and he grasped the Magician's hands and thanked him.

" 'Now,' said the Magician, 'you will find Grandmother up at the top of the hill and I wish you to take this medicine to her so that she will become as young as you are.'

" 'Thank you, thank you,' the young-old man replied, 'but what is Granny doing way up at the little stingy Gnome's house? She knows well that the little Gnome will never help us, he always runs and hides. He has always done that ever since I was a boy!'

"Then the Magician laughed and told the man all about watching the Gnome hide. 'And,' he went on, 'you and Grandmother may have the little Gnome's place to live in, for the little Gnome will never be able to leave his hiding-place in the vines.'

"So the Magician shook hands with the man and told him good-by and watched the man as he scampered up the hill with the medicine in his hands for his wife.

"After a year had passed a poorly-dressed woman climbed the hill which used to belong to the little Gnome and knocked at the door.

"'Come right in!' two cheery voices cried, and as the poorly dressed woman walked in, the little lady, who had been a little old woman before the Magician gave her the medicine, and her husband ran to meet the poorly-dressed stranger. 'Are you hungry?' they asked, and not waiting for an answer they ran to the cupboard and brought out food and drink.

"Then the poorly-dressed woman threw off her cloak and bonnet and the two saw it was their old friend the Magician.

"'Ha, ha, ha! That was a good joke on you,' he laughed. 'I wanted to see how you treated visitors.'

58

"The little man and the little lady laughed with the Magician and said: 'After you made us so happy, you don't believe that we could ever be anything but pleased to help others all we can.'

"'Well, I am glad of that,' the Magician laughed, 'for there's so much more fun in being helpful and generous than there is in being stingy.'

"'Indeed, we have found that out!' said the little lady.

"And they talked and visited with the Magician for a long time.

"Then just before the Magician left them, the little lady ran out to the garden and back again. 'We have found the little weazened-up Gnome!' she cried.

"'That's strange!' the Magician replied. 'I never knew my magic to fail and I said that he would disappear forever.'

" 'Oh, excuse me,' the little lady replied. 'You said, "May the little Gnome remain hidden forever amongst the vines!" and he is truly well hidden.'

"Then she held up a peanut, like this," said Orphant Annie. "And she broke it open, like this!" Orphant Annie cracked the peanut she held in her hand. "Then the little lady took the kernel from the peanut like this and split the kernel in two, like this!" Orphant Annie held up the two pieces of the kernel. "And there hiding between the two pieces of the peanut kernel was the little weazened-up Gnome!"

"Let's see, Orphant Annie!" the children cried. "Is it really there?"

"Sure," Orphant Annie answered, "every peanut you open you will find the little Gnome hiding between the kernels."

And when the children looked, they found this to be true.

VIII

THE PIXIE PLAY PARK

"MRS. GEORGIANA GROUNDHOG lives over in the large meadow, near the rail fence," said Orphant Annie, "but she is rather shy about coming out of her house when grown-up folks are about. However, sometimes we get a glimpse of her when she makes a trip to the market for green vegetables, and we often see where she has helped herself to some of our garden truck!"

"The Hired Man said yesterday, he was going to spend a whole day sometime, sitting behind the fence with a twenty-two rifle!" said Carl.

"Well, he just won't!" Orphant Annie laughed. "For I have hidden the rifle. He told me the same thing."

"Why does he want to shoot the Groundhogs?" Bessie asked.

"Well, you see," Orphant Annie answered, "the Hired Man naturally wants the garden to be as nice as possible and Mrs. Georgiana Groundhog and Mr. George Groundhog and the Groundhog children sometimes muss the garden up a good deal!"

"Shucks!" Carl exclaimed, "what difference does it make? We always have more than we can use anyway and stuff is left in the garden that just lays there and spoils!"

"You are right, Carl," Orphant Annie laughed, "but the Hired Man does not think of that. Why, when Georgiana Groundhog says to one of the Groundhog boys, 'Willie, take the basket and run over to the garden and bring back some vegetables,' Willie Groundhog hustles about his errand with his little Groundhog heart beating as happily as any real for sure, grown-up boy's, when he is doing something nice to help his mother. And if, when he runs to the garden, he sees a great big Hired Man rise up from behind the fence with something in his hands that makes a great bang, you can imagine just how frightened Willie becomes. You see, the Groundhogs do not know that the Hired Man plants the vegetables in the garden. The Groundhogs think they just grow there for every one who cares to take them. So they don't know it is stealing when they take the vegetables!"

"I wonder what Groundhogs do to amuse themselves?" Carl asked.

"Oh, don't worry," laughed Orphant Annie, "they have lots of fun, and that is what I started out to tell you. You know, nearly all animals can see much better than we can, for Mother Nature has given them very keen eyes. So they often see Fairies and Pixies and Dwarfs and Elves and Gnomes and everything like that; and it is quite easy for Georgiana Groundhog to see a Pixie, if the Pixie wishes to be seen.

"Well, one day a Pixie did wish to be seen, for he walked right up to Georgiana Groundhog's doorway where she was sweeping and said: 'Good morning, Georgiana Groundhog. It's a nice day, isn't it?'

A Pixie walked right up to Georgiana Groundhog's doorway where she was
sweeping and said, "Good morning, Georgiana Groundhog"

"And Georgiana Groundhog looked around and saw the dear little Pixie and she said: 'Good morning, cunning little Pixie! Yes, it is a lovely day.'

"And the Pixie dug his little toe in the soft ground as if he wanted to ask something but was shy about doing it. So Georgiana Groundhog laughed a little Groundhog laugh and asked: 'What is it you want, little Pixie?'

"Then the little Pixie laughed a little Pixie laugh and said: 'I'd like a piece of bread and butter with sugar on it.'

"So Georgiana Groundhog leaned her broom against the front door and said, 'Come around to the kitchen, Mr. Pixie, and I'll see what we can find!'

"Then Georgiana Groundhog led the way to the kitchen and opened the cupboard door. 'Which would you rather have, Mister Pixie?' Georgiana Groundhog asked, 'bread and butter with sugar on it, or bread and butter with honey on it, or bread and butter with raspberry jelly on it?'

"The little Pixie fidgeted around as if he were embarrassed, so Georgiana Groundhog laughed again and said, 'Now, Mister Pixie, you just sit on that chair and I'll fix you a piece of bread and butter with sugar on it, and a piece of bread and butter with honey on it, and a piece of bread and butter with raspberry jelly on it!' And that is what she did.

"Then she gave the little Pixie a glass of spring water and when he had eaten the three pieces of bread, she washed the raspberry jelly from around his mouth and asked him: 'Have you had enough?'

"And the little Pixie said, 'Yes, thank you, and it was very, very good, too.'

" 'I'm glad you liked it,' Georgiana Groundhog said.

" 'I guess I'll go home now,' replied the little Pixie.

" 'Where do you live?' Georgiana Groundhog asked him.

" 'Would you like to see where I live?' the little Pixie asked in reply. And when Georgiana Groundhog exclaimed,

'Yes indeedy!' the little Pixie said: 'All right, then come along.'

"But just as they left the house, here came George Groundhog and Willie Groundhog and Winnie Groundhog.

"'Where are you going?' they all asked Georgiana Groundhog.

"'This dear little Pixie is taking me to see where he lives,' answered Georgiana Groundhog.

"'They may go along too if they like,' the Pixie said.

"So the whole Groundhog family went with the Pixie to see where he lived.

"Well," Orphant Annie laughed, "you would never guess where the Pixie took them, so I will have to tell you. He took them through the rail fence and over to the brook, then he tapped upon a large stone near the brook and the large stone raised up in the air and they all went down a stairway that led beneath the ground in under the brook. 'Any time

65

you wish to come to see me,' said the Pixie, 'you must come to the stone and knock three times while you say to yourself: "Higgeldy-piggeldy!"'

"Then the Pixie led the Groundhog family down a roadway, under the ground, to a dear little house, just the kind of house you would expect a cunning little Pixie to live in. 'Here we are!' said the Pixie. 'Help yourself to any thing you see that you may care to have and I will be out in a minute.'

"So the Groundhog family walked about the Pixie garden and were so surprised at what they saw, you might have knocked their eyes off with a stick. The first thing they came to in the garden was a long row of bushes. The bushes were all different, for on one bush were pretty little red and blue and yellow and green slippers. On another bush there were stockings; on another little pairs of pants; on another, little dresses; on another bush there were bonnets; on another hats.

And so something to wear grew on all the bushes, neckties and everything, and all the Groundhogs had to do was to pick the slippers, stockings, pants and dresses and bonnets and hats that fitted them, and the first thing you knew, they were dressed so prettily they hardly knew themselves.

"Then when the little Pixie came out he was so pleased to see they had helped themselves that he told them the Pixies always grew the clothes for little creatures of the fields and forests, and led them out the back garden gate and into what looked like a large Fair Ground, for there were shows and swings and candy booths and pop-corn places and peanut-brittle shops and lemonade stands and ice-cream soda fountains and roller-coasters and merry-go-rounds, and everything. Not large ones like we have, but small ones for the little creatures of the fields and forests. And there, riding on the merry-go-rounds and roller-coasters and eating ice-cream and lollypops, were hundreds of little creatures, playing together and having the nicest time. 'You see,' said the little Pixie, 'all of the creatures here have been invited by the Pixies, and it is a Pixie law that there must be no fighting or quarreling, nor must any creature harm another while in Pixie Land!'

"And sure enough, the happy Groundhog family saw that old Mister Fox was having the nicest time riding on the merry-go-round with Mrs. Rabbit, and Winifred Weazel was showing two little Chipmunk boys all around the great Amusement Park.

" 'Now I must leave you,' said Pixie to the Groundhog family, 'and go bring others here, so have as much fun as you possibly can and when you get ready to leave just walk to the spot where you came in and say what I told you to say at the stone. Then you can go back home!'

"So Georgiana Groundhog and George Groundhog and Willie and Winnie Groundhog all thanked the dear little Pixie and asked him to come see them. And then they went among all the other little creatures and ate everything they wanted to eat and drank ice-cream sodas and rode on the merry-go-rounds and roller-coasters until it was time to go home.

"After that, whenever they wish to, the Groundhogs go to the large stone and say 'Higgeldy-piggeldy' and walk down the steps into the Pixies' land of play with the little creatures. And of course, few grown-ups know about the Pixie Land, so think that some of the little creatures of the fields and forests do not have any amusement.

"And the chances are," said Orphant Annie, "that when we think the little creatures are hiding in their little houses during the daytime, they are really down in Pixie Land playing together and forgetting all about the troubles they may have above the ground."

"I'd like to take a peep into the Pixies' Land, wouldn't you?" Carl asked Bessie and Orphant Annie.

"Yes," Bessie replied, "I'd like to ride on a roller-coaster right now and have a great big ice-cream soda."

"It must look cute to see all the little animals dressed in the Pixie clothes playing about in the Pixie Amusement Park," said Carl.

"Indeed it must be a very pleasant place for the little animals to go," Orphant Annie mused, as she looked dreamily across the meadow toward Georgiana Groundhog's burrow. "For, according to the Pixie laws, they must all be friends while in the Pixie Land. And to be with friends is in itself a great happiness."

IX

THE THINGAMAJIG AND THE WHATCHAMACALLIT

"THE Thingamajig and the Whatchamacallit once had an argument as to which one was right," said Orphant Annie, as she held the new pup under the pump while Carl pumped the water over him. "The Thingamajig said that fleas hopped and the Whatchamacallit said that fleas jumped.

"Here, now! don't you do that!" Orphant Annie cried, as the puppy wiggled and twisted to get out from under the water spout. "You have to get your bath. There, that's enough, Carl. Now hand me the soap, please.

"Well, sir," Orphant Annie said, as she rubbed the new puppy dog's back with the soap and covered him with the lather, "the Thingamajig and the Whatchamacallit argued and argued until they grew tired, then they rested and thought up new things to say to each other, then they would start all over again and argue until it was time to go to bed.

"And the more they argued the more they became convinced that each was right and that the other would never be able to prove to him that he was mistaken. It would have been all right if the Thingamajig and the Whatchamacallit had not been such good friends and had not lived in the same house and slept in the same bed; they probably would have forgotten all about the argument after they separated the first time.

"But living together as they did and always being together when they went out, the argument continued for weeks and weeks.

"Why, whenever they went down to the Wheeswiggle grocery store and sat around the cracker barrel, instead of visiting with the neighbors as they should have done, they argued and argued. Well, it finally got so that whenever the Thingamajig and the Whatchamacallit came in the Wheeswiggle grocery store, the Snipdooly and the Gringweez always put away the checker-board and went outside until the two had finished their argument.

"But as the Thingamajig and the Whatchamacallit always stayed and argued around the cracker barrel until the Wheeswiggle closed for the night, it finally got so the other neighbors would peep into the store first and if the Thingamajig and the Whatchamacallit were there, the neighbors would all go down to the Jinxwhang's barber shop or some other place and visit together.

"Well, sir, one day a new family moved into the cave around the corner from the Wheeswiggle grocery and that evening the head of the new family came into the store to sit around the cracker barrel and get acquainted with his neighbors. And he had not been there long before the Thingamajig and the Whatchamacallit came in and sat down. 'Good evening!' said the Snarlygig,—that was the newcomer's name. And the Thingamajig and the Whatchamacallit said

The Thingamajig and the Whatchamacallit argued and argued

good evening to him and then started their argument all over again.

"'I tell you, Whatchamacallit, you are wrong!' cried the Thingamajig.

"'I tell you I'm right and it is you who are wrong!' the Whatchamacallit replied, as he reached in the cracker barrel and took a handful of crackers.

"'I tell you that I AM right!' cried the Thingamajig, as he, too, reached into the cracker barrel and took a handful of crackers.

"'It looks like it might rain to-morrow,' said the Snarlygig, as he reached into the cracker barrel and took a handful of crackers.

"'They jump!' cried the Whatchamacallit with his mouth full of crackers.

"'They hop!' cried the Thingamajig with his mouth full of crackers.

"'How can they hop, when you know that they jump!' cried the Whatchamacallit, as he reached into the cracker barrel and took another handful of crackers.

"'How can they jump, when they hop?' cried the Thingamajig, as he took another handful of crackers from the cracker barrel.

"'It is clouding up as if it might storm to-night!' said the Snarlygig, as he reached into the cracker barrel and took another handful of crackers.

"'They jump, anyway!' cried the Whatchamacallit, with his mouth full of crackers.

"'They hop, anyway!' cried the Thingamajig, with his mouth full of crackers.

"'What are you talking about?' the Snarlygig asked, with his mouth full of crackers.

"'Fleas!' said the Thingamajig.

"'Fleas!' said the Whatchamacallit.

"'The Whatchamacallit says that fleas jump!' said the Thingamajig, as he reached into the box of prunes and took a handful.

" 'The Thingamajig says that fleas hop," cried the Whatchamacallit, as he reached into the prune box and took a handful of prunes.

" 'And they *do,*' cried the Thingamajig excitedly.

" 'And they *don't!*' cried the Whatchamacallit excitedly. 'They jump!'

" 'Oh, that's it, is it?' the Snarlygig laughed, as he reached into the prune box and took a handful of prunes. 'Well, well! Ha, ha, ha!'

" 'What are you laughing at?' asked the Thingamajig.

" 'He's laughing at you,' cried the Whatchamacallit. 'He knows fleas jump.'

" 'He's laughing at *you!*' cried the Thingamajig. 'He knows fleas hop!'

" 'Ha, ha, ha!' laughed the Snarlygig. 'You're both wrong, fleas skip.'

" 'Dear me!' said the Thingamajig.

" 'Land sakes!' said the Whatchamacallit.

" 'Oh, yes,' said the Snarlygig, as he reached into the prune box and took another handful of prunes. 'Every one knows that fleas skip. Yes, yes, indeed.'

" 'I knew they did,' said the Thingamajig and the Whatchamacallit together, 'but I didn't want to let on that I knew it.'

"So the Thingamajig and the Whatchamacallit shook hands and agreed never to argue again, and went home.

"When they got home, the Thingamajig said, 'I knew all along that fleas jumped.' And the Whatchamacallit said, 'And I knew all along that fleas hopped, and we have just been contrary, and all about some silly little thing, too.'

" 'Yes,' replied the Thingamajig, 'and I am ashamed of myself.'

" 'And I am ashamed of myself, too,' said the Whatchamacallit.

"And," Orphant Annie finished as she wiped the new puppy dog's back with a cloth, "the Thingamajig and the Whatchamacallit each took a pot of red paint and each painted a wide smile across the other's face. You see they were so sorry for having been stubborn they did not feel like smiling for a week. So that's why you always see a Thingamajig and a Whatchamacallit with a wide smile painted across his face."

"Yes, but we've never seen a Thingamajig or a Whatchamacallit," laughed Carl and Bessie.

"Well, neither have I," Orphant Annie laughed, "but maybe we will some day.

"Now look at that, will you?" she went on as the new puppy dog was released after his bath and ran out in the dusty road and rolled over and over. "Isn't he just like a Whatchamacallit?"

"Just like a Thingamajig!" laughed Bessie.

X

HOW THE GRASSHOPPERS HELPED THE FAIRIES

"DID you ever notice how much a grasshopper looks like a horse?" Orphant Annie asked as she held a large yellow grasshopper up so the children could see it. "Look!" Orphant Annie continued. "It even has a horse's collar on!"

"Maybe grasshoppers are fairies' horses," ventured Bessie.

"Who knows?" Orphant Annie replied. "But I can tell you one thing, the grasshopper helped the fairies at one time when they needed help very much." And seeing the children wanted to hear the story, Orphant Annie began.

"Well, it was a long, long time ago, of course, that a family of cunning little fairies no larger than your little finger, lived together under a log in a great forest. Beneath the log, the fairies had scraped away the stones and built walls and passages down into the ground, so that it was nice and cool in summer and warm and cozy in the winter time. And it made no difference to the fairies how long the snow stayed on the ground, for there was a tiny chimney which led from

77

their little home up through a hole in the log to the air above. So in the winter time they had little crackly fires in the little fireplace which made their living-room bright and cozy and comfortable, even when Jack Frost snapped the twigs of the trees and pinched the ears and noses of the forest creatures that lived above ground.

"The tiny little fairies who lived beneath the log were very kindly little people and while they enjoyed having fun, they were never mischievous. In fact they seemed to get a great deal of amusement by doing generous, kindly acts for others. And so, all the little woodfolk who knew the fairies loved them very much.

"One time when the ground was frozen and the snow lay in patches through the forest and the little family of fairies was sitting down in its cozy little under-the-log-home, some one came through the forest and dragged away the log for firewood. Of course, whoever it was that did this, did not know that the log sheltered the little family of fairies, or they would have taken some other log. And as the fairies all ran deeper down into their underground home when the log was moved, no one saw them for a long time. Then when they came up to peep above ground to see what had disturbed their log, Witchy Crosspatch happened to be passing, and seeing the cunning little fairy people, she caught all except one and took them to her home. This would have been all right, had Witchy Crosspatch taken them home out of kindness, but that was far from her thoughts. Witchy Crosspatch thought to herself when she caught the little fairies, 'I can keep them until summer time and then sell them to people to have in side-shows.'

"For," continued Orphant Annie, "you know, any one would be very glad to pay five or ten pennies to see a cunning little fairy no larger than your little finger. Well, when Witchy Crosspatch reached home, she made a little box out

There is no telling what would have happened to them if it had not been for
the one little fairy who escaped from Witchy Crosspatch

of boards and put a padlock on it so that no one could open it except herself."

"Didn't she give them any food?" Carl asked.

"Oh, yes," Orphant Annie replied, "Witchy Crosspatch knew that the tiny little people would not last until summer time unless she fed them. But she only gave them bread crumbs, and lots and lots of nights she forgot to give them anything at all."

"She must have been very wicked and cruel," Bessie said, her heart swelling at the thought of any one mistreating such dear little cunning creatures.

"Indeed she was," Orphant Annie agreed. "But crosspatches always think more of themselves than of others, or they would not be crosspatches.

"But someway or other, even though they did not get the kind of food they were used to, the little fairy family lived in the wooden box until the warm sun melted the ice and snow, and the leaves and grasses became green in their summer dresses. Then Witchy Crosspatch caught the Epizoodick from eating too many toadstools and had to stay in her bed for days and days, so the tiny little fairies went without anything to eat at all.

"There is no telling what would have happened to them if it had not been for the one little fairy who had escaped from Witchy Crosspatch. I suppose in time the little creatures would have just dried up and withered away like rose petals in the box. But their little brother had not forgotten them, even though they did not know what had become of *him*. When Witchy Crosspatch caught the fairies and took them home, this little fairy had followed Witchy Crosspatch right in to her own house, and while Witchy Crosspatch did not even dream of it, he was living under her kitchen stove, just waiting for the time when he might find a way to rescue his brothers and sisters from the stuffy little box. Many a time at night, when Witchy Crosspatch was fast asleep the little fairy tried to unfasten the pad-lock on the box, but he could not do this without the key, and Witchy Crosspatch always wore the key around her neck. For like the distrustful person she was, she was always afraid some one might find the little fairies and take them from her.

"So when summer came, there was Witchy Crosspatch in bed with the Epizoodick and not able to get out of the house to sell the box of fairies to the circus men.

"The one little fairy who lived under Witchy Crosspatch's kitchen stove really felt sorry for Witchy Crosspatch because it is not very pleasant to have the Epizoodick even if you are a crosspatch, but he did not know what to do to help her. So he just stayed under the stove in the daytime and at night he always tried to open the lock on the box.

"One night, when Witchy Crosspatch had the Epizoodick worse than anything, the little fairy was trying to unfasten the lock on the box and he heard some one say: 'What in the world are you trying to do?' Looking around, he saw that a grasshopper had crawled under Witchy Crosspatch's kitchen door and was standing there watching him.

" 'I'm trying to unlock this box,' the little fairy answered when he saw that it was Georgie Grasshopper, 'for Witchy Crosspatch has locked all my brothers and sisters in it, and I am sure they must be very tired living in a stuffy box!'

" 'Yes, indeed, they must be uncomfortable!' Georgie Grasshopper said, and he scratched his head, trying to think of a way to help the little fairy rescue the other fairies. Finally Georgie Grasshopper scratched just the right spot on his head and so thought of a plan. 'Just you wait until I return!' he said to the little fairy. And Georgie Grasshopper crawled out under the kitchen door. Pretty soon he was back again, and with him came hundreds of his uncles and aunts and cousins and grandpas and grandmas, and Georgie Grasshopper jumped up on the wooden box and said, 'Now I will work until I get tired, then another Grasshopper can work until he gets tired and in a short time we will have all of the little fairies out of the box.'

"The little fairy wondered how Georgia Grasshopper expected to get the box opened but it did not take him very long to find out. See," said Orphant Annie as she held up the Grasshopper. "Each Grasshopper has queer long legs that look just like saws. And of course that is what Georgie Grasshopper thought of. So he sat down on the edge of the top of the box and used one leg as a saw until it grew tired, then he used the other leg and sawed away until it grew tired. When he had done this six or seven times, Georgie Grasshopper was ready for a rest, so another grasshopper jumped up on the box, took his place and sawed until he grew tired.

"It was fortunate that Witchy Crosspatch had made the box out of thin boards, for it was very hard work for the grasshoppers. But they were willing little workers and kept at it until they sawed a hole large enough for all the fairies to climb through. And it wasn't a very large hole either, for living only on bread crumbs had not by any means made the little fairies any fatter.

"My how glad they were to be out of the box. They hugged their little brother and then hugged all the grasshoppers, one after another.

" 'Where is the old Witchy Crosspatch who shut us up in the box?' they asked.

" 'She's in bed with the Epizoodick!' the little fairy told them.

" 'Then,' said the little fairies, 'we will get into the cupboard and eat and eat, for we are very hungry.' So the little fairies and the grasshoppers ran to the cupboard and ate and ate until they could not eat any more. Then they all lay down under the kitchen stove and took a long nap, for they had eaten so much it made them sleepy. They were all very tired, too, so they slept almost the whole day and night. And probably would have slept longer if Witchy Crosspatch's Epizoodick hadn't made her howl so loud. Of course, the howls made the little fairies jump and the grasshoppers scattered in all directions—jumpity, jumpity, jump.

"But when they found that Witchy Crosspatch could not get out of her bed, they all came back under the kitchen stove. 'My, how she howls!' said one grasshopper, 'she must have been eating green apples.'

" 'Maybe you'd howl, too,' said the little fairy, 'if you had the Epizoodick.'

83

" 'No, we wouldn't!' all the grasshoppers cried. 'We know just what to do for the Epizoodick!'

" 'What do you do?' all the little fairies asked, for now that they were out of Witchy Crosspatch's box and had all eaten as much as they could hold, they felt sorry for Witchy Crosspatch and easily forgave her for the way she had treated them.

" 'There's a great leaf growing in the fields,' said the grasshoppers, 'and you have to make a plaster of it and wrap up your big toe. Then in a day or two, you won't have the Epizoodick any more.'

" 'Then let's get the leaves and make the plaster,' said all the little fairies. But when they went to the kitchen door the little fairies found that they were just a wee bit too large to crawl out the little chink through which the grasshoppers crawled.

" 'Never mind,' the kind grasshoppers said, 'we will get the leaves and bring them to you.' So out the chink they crawled.

"But when they tried to get the big leaves through the chink, they found the chink was too small. There was only one way to do and that was for the grasshoppers to chew the large leaves into tiny bits and then crawl through the chink

and put the tiny bits on a rag which the fairies had found. When the grasshoppers had enough leaves chewed up, the fairies waited until Witchy Crosspatch went to sleep and then they hurried to tie the plaster of chewed-up leaves around her big toe.

" 'Now, she'll be all right in the morning,' the grasshoppers said, as they told the little fairies good-by and went out through the chink under the kitchen door. The little fairies wondered how they might get out of Witchy Crosspatch's house, but as they couldn't find a way, they decided they would visit the cupboard again. And in the morning when Witchy Crosspatch awakened she did not have even a smidgin of the Epizoodick, so she hopped out of bed happier than she had been for years and years. Then when she went to the kitchen and discovered all the little fairies curled up asleep under her kitchen stove, she knew in a minute who it was that had tied up her toe and cured her of the Epizoodick. So Witchy Crosspatch took up all the little fairies and carried them in her apron to their home and placed them right where the log had been. Then she tiptoed away, her heart beating pitty-pat for the kindness she had done. And it made her feel so good to have her heart seem as if it were full of sunshine, she decided right then and there that she would never be a crosspatch again, but would try her level best every day to do generous, kindly acts for others.

"And when they woke up, the little fairies wondered how they happened to be safe at home. And look!" said Orphant Annie, as she put one finger to the grasshopper's mouth and took it away covered with a brown liquid. "The grasshoppers chewed so many of the tobacco leaves when they cured Witchy Crosspatch of the Epizoodick, they caught the habit of chewing!"

"Do they still chew tobacco?" Carl asked.

"Lawsy no," Orphant Annie laughed. "They just chew grass and things like that for you know chewing tobacco is not a bit nice."

"Ah-ha!" a loud voice startled Orphant Annie and the children. "So it was you who took my tobacco, Orphant Annie!" And the Hired Man shook his long forefinger at her.

"Yes, I did!" Orphant Annie laughed. "And I threw it away. You ought to be ashamed to chew tobacco."

"Well!" the Hired Man said, as he shrugged his shoulders and shuffled back around the house. "I'll try going without it a mite longer, but I reckon I'll be chawin' corn-silk 'fore the day's out!"

Orphant Annie put the grasshopper down upon a broad leaf and winked at the children. "Come on in and watch me make some doughnuts!" she said. "We'll see if we can't get him something better than corn-silk to chew."

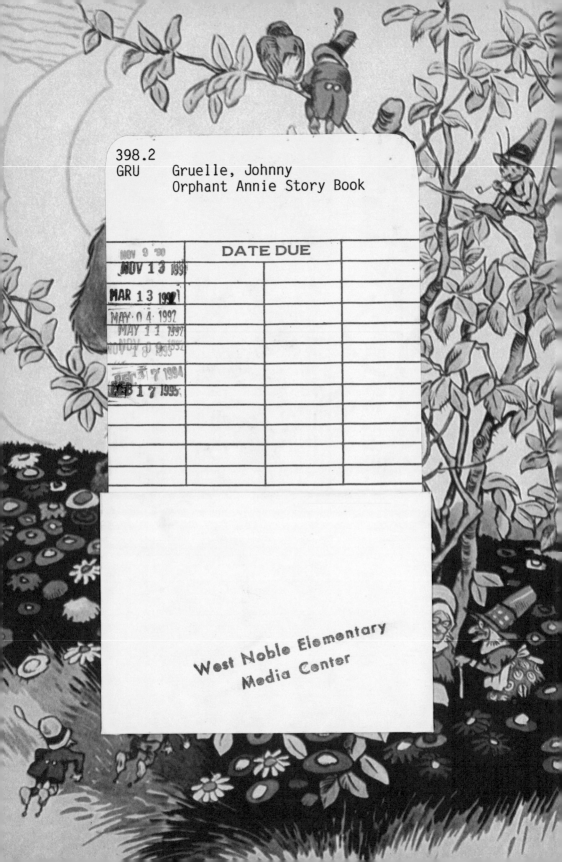

398.2
GRU   Gruelle, Johnny
          Orphant Annie Story Book

NOV 9 '90	DATE DUE		
NOV 13 1991			
MAR 13 1992			
MAY 04 1992			
MAY 11 1992			
NOV 18 1993			
DEC 17 1994			
FEB 17 1995			